W9-ABZ-078

Listen to the Desert
Oye al desierto

by Pat Mora
Illustrated by Francisco X. Mora

CLARION BOOKS / *New York*

Clarion Books
a Houghton Mifflin Company imprint
215 Park Avenue South, New York, NY 10003
Text copyright © 1994 by Pat Mora
Illustrations copyright © 1994 by Francisco X. Mora

Illustrations executed in watercolor
on 330-lb. cold press Lanaquarelle paper.
Text is 22-point Meridien.

Printed in China

www.houghtonmifflinbooks.com

Library of Congress Cataloging-in-Publication Data

Mora, Pat.
    Listen to the desert – Oye al desierto / by Pat Mora ; illustrated
by Francisco X. Mora.
        p.   cm.
    Summary: A bilingual poem which describes some of the sounds
of nature in a desert.
    ISBN 0-395-67292-9 PA ISBN 0-618-11144-1
    1. Deserts—Juvenile poetry. 2. Animals sounds—Juvenile
poetry. 3. Children's poetry, American. [1. Deserts—Poetry.
2. Animal sounds—Poetry. 3. American poetry. 4. Spanish language
materials—Bilingual.] I. Mora, Francisco X., ill. II. Title. III. Title:
Oye al desierto
PS3563.O73L57   1994
811'.54—dc20
                               93-31463
                               CIP
                               AC

SCP 20 19 18 17 16 15 14 13 12

To my son, Bill,
who helped me see the desert anew
— *P. M.*

For my mother,
always ready to tell me a story
— *F. M.*

Listen to the desert, pon, pon, pon.
Listen to the desert, pon, pon, pon.
Oye al desierto, pon, pon, pon.
Oye al desierto, pon, pon, pon.

Listen to the owl hoot, whoo, whoo, whoo.
Listen to the owl hoot, whoo, whoo, whoo.
Oye la lechuza, uuu, uuu, uuu.
Oye la lechuza, uuu, uuu, uuu.

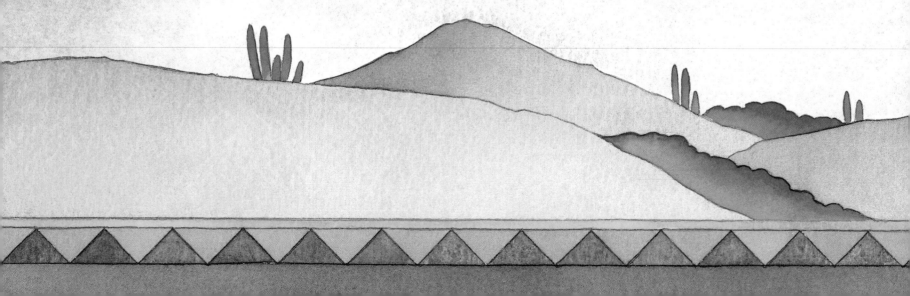

Listen to the toad hop, plop, plop, plop.
Listen to the toad hop, plop, plop, plop.
Oye al sapito, plap, plap, plap.
Oye al sapito, plap, plap, plap.

Listen to the snake hiss, tst-tst-tst, tst-tst-tst.
Listen to the snake hiss, tst-tst-tst, tst-tst-tst.
Silba la culebra, ssst, ssst, ssst.
Silba la culebra, ssst, ssst, ssst.

Listen to the dove say coo, coo, coo.
Listen to the dove say coo, coo, coo.
La paloma arrulla, currucú, currucú, currucú.
La paloma arrulla, currucú, currucú, currucú.

Listen to coyote call, ar-ar-aooo, ar-ar-aooo.
Listen to coyote call, ar-ar-aooo, ar-ar-aooo.
El coyote canta, ahúúú, ahúúú, ahúúú.
El coyote canta, ahúúú, ahúúú, ahúúú.

Listen to the fish eat, puh, puh, puh.
Listen to the fish eat, puh, puh, puh.
Oye pescaditos, plaf, plaf, plaf.
Oye pescaditos, plaf, plaf, plaf.

Listen to the mice say scrrt, scrrt, scrrt.
Listen to the mice say scrrt, scrrt, scrrt.
Oye ratoncitos, criic, criic, criic.
Oye ratoncitos, criic, criic, criic.

Listen to the rain dance, plip, plip, plip.
Listen to the rain dance, plip, plip, plip.
La lluvia baila, baila, plin, plin, plin.
La lluvia baila, baila, plin, plin, plin.

Listen to the wind spin, zoom, zoom, zoom.
Listen to the wind spin, zoom, zoom, zoom.
Oye, zumba el viento, zuum, zuum, zuum.
Oye, zumba el viento, zuum, zuum, zuum.

Listen to the desert, pon, pon, pon.
Listen to the desert, pon, pon, pon.
Oye al desierto, pon, pon, pon.
Oye al desierto, pon, pon, pon.

[SPANISH]
E
MO
4/11/07
7:00